Yael Plants Seeds

by Malky Weinstock
illustrated by Steve Pileggi

This book is dedicated in loving memory to our unforgettable
Mother, Grandmother and Great-Grandmother

Mrs. Genendl bas Rav Shlomo Berkowitz, *zt"l*

Whose attributes, bravery, contentment, diligence, devotion, exertions, frugality,
gentleness, humaneness, love, intelligence, perseverance, quiet demeanor,
righteousness, simplicity, sincerity, tenacity, uniqueness, work ethic and wisdom
continue to inspire, motivate and energize our lives as we endeavor to walk in her
balanced path of דרך הממוצע.

Avrohom Pinchas and Mindy Berkowitz,
children and grandchildren, עמו"ש

Published by Lite Girl, Inc.
Text and illustrations © 2019 by Lite Girl, Inc.
www.bealitegirl.com

For updates, news, events, previews and special
introductory offers on new exciting LITE Girl book
releases and other products, sign up for FREE
membership now at www.bealitegirl.com

ISBN: 978-1-60763-289-4

Distributed by:
The Judaica Press, Inc.
www.judaicapress.com
800.972.6201

Summary: Nature is one of the glorious miracles of
Hashem, as Yael discovers when she and her Savta
plant tomato seeds. Yael can't imagine how her seeds
will grow when buried underground —until several
weeks later she is surprised to find magnificent
cherry tomato vines growing! Enhance your child's
love of Hashem by appreciating His wonders!

Illustrations: Steve Pileggi/Blue Lion Designs
Editor: N. Shapiro
Narration recording, background music, & song lyrics:
    ReaL Sound Studio
Singer: Dovy Werner

Manufactured in China

"Savta, what are you doing?!"

Yael was playing in Savta's backyard when she
noticed Savta wearing a sun hat and gloves ...
and doing something new and different!

3

"Today ... I'm planting cherry
tomatoes!" Savta said happily.

"See, here's the package!"

Yael's eyes
opened wide.

Yael was confused.
"Are tomatoes going to
grow from the package?"

Savta laughed as she
put a little brown
thing in Yael's hand.

"What's this?" Yael
asked, turning it
over and over.

It didn't look like
a cherry tomato.
It didn't look like
much of anything.

"It's a tomato seed!"
Savta explained.

"A tomato plant will grow from this tiny seed!
But first ... we have to put it in the ground."

Savta cleared a spot in the garden with her little
shovel and showed Yael how to press the tiny seed
into the ground. Savta marked the place with
a little flag. "Plant some more," Savta sang.

Savta showed Yael how to pour water over the seeds. Then Savta covered all the seeds with dirt.

"How will my tiny seeds grow?" Yael asked. "They're all covered up!"

"Oh, don't worry, Yael," Savta said gently. "You know who will take care of your tiny seeds and help them grow into beautiful plants?

"Hashem! It's one of the amazing things only Hashem can do!"

Yael bent over, looking closely.
"Can I watch them grow?" she asked.

"*Im yirtzeh Hashem*, our seeds *will* grow, Yael!" Savta said.
"But first they will need lots of sun and rain."

That night, Yael called Mindy. "My Savta and I planted tomatoes today!" she told Mindy excitedly.

The next day, Yael asked Mommy
if they could stop by Savta's house.

When they got there,
Yael ran straight to the backyard.

But the garden was still empty.
Where were her tomatoes?

Yael went inside and asked Savta,
"Why don't I see the tomatoes yet?"

"It will take some time," Savta said. "First, the
rain must come to help our plants grow."

When Yael waited for her bus the next morning,
clouds filled the sky and the rain began pouring
down. *Splash, splash!* Everything was getting
wet. But Yael didn't mind. Savta had told her
the rain would help her tomato seeds grow!

Yael came home from school in the pouring rain.
Shaking the rain from her hair, Yael called Savta.
"Savta, isn't it great for our plants that it's raining?"

"Yes!" said Savta. "With the rain, Hashem is helping
our seeds start to grow! The rain helps them sprout
roots under the ground. You can't see the roots,
but they will keep our tomato plants attached
to the ground so they can grow really tall!"

The next week, Yael checked again. Small green leaves were growing in the spots she had planted her tiny seeds. "Those must be the plants ... but there are no tomatoes!" Yael said sadly.

"This is just the start," Savta assured her. "They will grow much more, and then you'll see the tomatoes we are waiting for!"

15

Things got busy for Yael. Soon the
school year was ending, and they were
preparing for their Pre-1a graduation!

There were lots of songs to learn,
and graduation hats to make ....

Yael forgot all about the seeds
she and Savta had planted.

"Let's bring your graduation
invitation to show Saba and Savta,"
said Mommy one day, a few weeks later.
The whole family piled into the car.

The weather was beautiful — a lovely, warm,
late spring day. "Why don't you take Baby
Esther out to play in the backyard a bit?"
Savta told Yael with a gleam in her eye.

Yael took Esther into the backyard garden,
and there she saw ... a sight she couldn't believe!

A row of beautiful vines — fully grown!

And bunches — more than she could count —
of the most beautiful, round, bite-size,
deliciously red cherry tomatoes!

She stared and stared in wonder.
It looked like a big tomato party!

21

Little Esther crawled off and picked
a little tomato. She laughed and giggled,
squishing the tomato in her little hand.
Tomato juice ran down her arm!
"Ball-ee, ball-ee!" she said. "More, more!"

Just then everybody
came into the yard.

"Look, look!" Yael cried.
"Our tiny seeds grew into
these plants with tons of
these cutie tomatoes!
I can't wait to bring some
for show and tell!"

"Baby Esther is very excited about them, too!"
laughed Mommy as she scooped her up.

"Yes, it's a great idea for show and tell!" Savta said.
"You can show your class our beautiful tomatoes.
Then you can tell them about Hashem's incredible
wonders — how He made them grow from tiny seeds!

Wouldn't you like to tell your friends
about Hashem's amazing world, too?

Here are the Yael Plants Seeds song lyrics. Hope you'll sing along!
And remember, you can be a LITE GIRL, too!

(You can listen to the song being played on the Yael Plants Seeds CD.)

How do vegetables grow in a garden?
They come from a tiny seed.
A red tomato — how does that happen? —
A miracle it must be …

CHORUS:
We know it is all miracles,
Fantastic, amazing miracles,
From the one and only Hashem.
Oh, it's a world of miracles,
Most amazing miracles,
From the one and only Hashem.

How does water get to a seed where
We know there's no kitchen sink? (In a garden!)
I stop and wonder, when all of the sudden
I feel droplets — it's raining.

CHORUS

Pick a delicious fruit off from its tree —
An apple, a juicy peach —
Notice its colors, its shape, and its form,
Designed by Hashem perfectly.

CHORUS X 3

A miracle!

Also in the LITE Girl Series ...

A lite girl BOOK

Yael's Loving World

by Malky Weinstock
illustrated by Steve Pileggi

love·inspire·teach·encourage

A lite girl BOOK

New Shoes for Yael

Audio/ Musical CD Included!

by Malky Weinstock
illustrated by Steve Pileggi

love·inspire·teach·encourage

A lite girl BOOK

Yael Becomes a Giver

Audio/ Musical CD Included!

by Malky Weinstock
illustrated by Steve Pileggi

love·inspire·teach·encourage

Yael Worries No More

Audio/ Musical CD Included!

by Malky Weinstock
illustrated by Steve Pileggi

love·inspire·teach·encourage

A lite girl BOOK

Yael Gets A Guest

Audio/ Musical CD Included!

by Malky Weinstock
illustrated by Steve Pileggi

love·inspire·teach·encourage

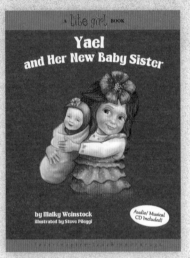

A lite girl BOOK

Yael and Her New Baby Sister

by Malky Weinstock
illustrated by Steve Pileggi

Audio/ Musical CD Included!

love·inspire·teach·encourage

A lite girl BOOK

Yael's Great Big Family

Audio/ Musical CD Included!

by Malky Weinstock
illustrated by Steve Pileggi

love·inspire·teach·encourage

A lite girl BOOK

Yael and the Shabbos Treats

by Malky Weinstock
illustrated by Steve Pileggi

Audio/Musical CD Included!

love·inspire·teach·encourage

A lite girl BOOK

Yael Keeps On Trying

by Malky Weinstock
illustrated by Steve Pileggi

Audio/Musical CD Included!

love·inspire·teach·encourage